THE RENEGADES.

DEFENDERS OF THE PLANET

ARCTIC MELTDOWN

DK LONDON

Senior Editor Ashwin Khurana
Designer Kit Lane
Editor Vicky Richards
US Editor Jennette ElNaggar
Managing Editor Francesca Baines
Managing Art Editor Philip Letsu
Production Editor Kavita Varma
Senior Production Controller Jude Crozier
Jacket Designer Surabhi Wadhwa-Gandhi
Jacket Design Development Manager Sophia MTT
Publisher Andrew Mcintyre
Associate Publishing Director Liz Wheeler
Art Director Karen Self
Publishing Director Jonathan Metcalf

First American Edition, 2020
Published in the United States by DK Publishing
1450 Broadway, Suite 801, New York, NY 10018

A catalog record for this book
is available from the Library of Congress.
ISBN 978-0-7440-2454-8 (Paperback)
ISBN 978-0-7440-3250-5 (ALB)

Printed and bound in China

For the curious
www.dk.com

MIX
Paper from
responsible sources
FSC™ C018179

This book was made with
Forest Stewardship Council® certified paper—
one small step in DK's commitment to a sustainable future.
For more information go to www.dk.com/our-green-pledge

THE RENEGADES.

DEFENDERS OF THE PLANET

CREATED BY JEREMY BROWN, KATY JAKEWAY,
ELLENOR MERERID, LIBBY REED,
AND DAVID SELBY

ARCTIC MELTDOWN

WHAT ON EARTH IS THAT?!

THIS...THIS IS IMPOSSIBLE--WHERE DID IT COME FROM?! DO ANOTHER SCAN FOR ANY HEAT SIGNATURES.

RUNNING SCAN, PROFESSOR. THERE APPEAR TO BE SIGNIFICANT HEAT READINGS BELOW YOU, AS WELL AS AN UNUSUAL CONCENTRATION OF METHANE.

OH MY! WE'RE GOING TO NEED A BIGGER SCANNER...

MY FIANCÉ LIVED OVERSEAS, AND I WAS GOING TO JOIN HIM, BUT...HE PASSED AWAY.

I NEED TO FLY OUT FOR THE FUNERAL, AS THERE'S NO OTHER WAY I CAN GET THERE IN TIME. AND IT'S NOT JUST ME--THERE ARE LOTS OF PEOPLE THAT COULD BE HURT BY YOUR ACTIONS--

--AND THEY AREN'T BAD--THEY'RE JUST PEOPLE, LEON.

I...AMBER, I'M SORRY. I HAD NO IDEA. I DIDN'T EVEN THINK OR CONSIDER... ANYTHING LIKE THAT, HONESTLY.

BUT YOU'RE RIGHT--MY FIGHT ISN'T AGAINST PEOPLE JUST TRYING TO LIVE AS BEST AS THEY CAN WITH WHAT THEY... WELL, WHAT WE'VE ALL BEEN DEALT.

SO WILL YOU GO THROUGH WITH IT?

NO...I THINK I'LL DO SOMETHING DIFFERENT...

I THINK WE SHOULD SCRAP THE DRONES...YEAH, YOU HEARD ME RIGHT. I WAS THINKING A LESS...AGGRESSIVE AND MORE PEACEFUL OPTION INSTEAD...

...YES, THIS IS REALLY LEON SPEAKING.

--AND THANK YOU ALL FOR YOUR TIME!

WAIT...IS THAT...?

...JASON GREENLEAF!

FLY GREEN. FLY GREENLEAF

WE HOPE TO SEE YOU BOARDING ONE OF OUR PLANES FOR YOUR NEXT TRIP--

GREENLEAF

--AND WE GUARANTEE YOU THE MOST ENJOYABLE, RELAXING EXPERIENCE--MADE ALL THE *GREENER* BY OUR BIOFUELS AND *IMPROVED* ENGINES--

--MAKING YOUR TRIP NOT ONLY *CHEAPER* BUT *MORE ECO-FRIENDLY* THAN ANY OTHER AIRLINE!

COME ON, WE NEED TO GO TO OUR GATE *NOW*.

FLY GREE

GREENLEAF

HUH? UH, SURE...

13

EVERYONE WHO HAS COME HERE HAS BROUGHT SOMETHING NEW. WE DIDN'T HIDE--WE WORKED TOGETHER. THAT'S SOMETHING I THINK YOU TWO COULD DO WITH LEARNING!

THANK YOU. I...I DON'T THINK WE EVER ASKED YOUR NAME?

OF COURSE, MY NAME IS ESHE.

I'M MO.

KATELYN.

ESHE? WE HAVE A FRIEND BACK IN THE UK. WE LOST CONTACT DURING THE FIRE. IS THERE ANY WAY WE CAN LET HIM KNOW WE'RE OKAY?

HMM. WELL, COMMUNICATIONS WITH THE OUTSIDE WORLD ARE PRETTY LIMITED AT THE MOMENT. BUT I'LL SEE WHAT I CAN DO.

KNOCK
KNOCK

OH, FOR-- LEON, I TOLD YOU, IT'S OVER. GO HOME.

SHILPA, I'M--

"TURNING OVER A NEW LEAF"? YES, YOU ALWAYS ARE! BUT I'M DONE WITH YOUR ERRATIC BEHAVIOR, HAVING TO BE YOUR THERAPIST--

I'M NOT HERE FOR THAT, SHILPA. I'M HERE BECAUSE I NEED YOUR HELP.

WELL... I SUPPOSE YOU'D BETTER COME IN THEN.

PRIME MINISTER

SO IT TURNS OUT THIS GUY, JASON GREENLEAF, IS A COMPLETE FRAUD! IN MAKING HIS BIOFUELS, HE'S THROWING PEOPLE OFF THEIR LAND TO BUILD PLANTATIONS.

AND IF HE KEEPS GOING...WELL, LET'S JUST SAY BAD THINGS WILL HAPPEN...

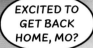

EXCITED TO GET BACK HOME, MO?

OH, SURE. I'VE BEEN GETTING BORED OF ALL THE HOT WEATHER AND STUNNING WILDLIFE ANYWAY...

SO WHILE WE WERE IN KULANDU, WE EXTRACTED THE DNA OF A NATIVE SPECIES OF CHAMELEON.

LONDON, UNOFFICIAL APOCO-FEAR ANONYMOUS MEETING

THEY SHED THEIR SKIN, SO THE LITTLE GUY WASN'T HARMED IN THE PROCESS.

HAVE YOU EVER LOOKED AT A CHAMELEON AND THOUGHT, "THAT WOULD BE AWESOME"-- BLENDING IN TO YOUR ENVIRONMENT AT WILL?

OF ALL THE SUPERPOWERS I COULD CHOOSE...INVISIBILITY ISN'T THE ONE I'D GO FOR.

WEIRDLY, NO.

WELL, NOW YOU CAN--CATCH!

YOU ALWAYS WERE VERY STUCK IN YOUR WAYS.

AND THIS ISN'T ABOUT YOU LIVING YOUR FANTASY. IT'S ABOUT YOU--WELL, ALL OF US--LEARNING SOMETHING, TRYING TO DO WHAT WE CAN... MAYBE NOT BEING SO STUBBORN.

EVERYTHING.

THE LONGER I KEEP THE SPECS ON... THE LONGER I CAN BEAR IT, THE FURTHER I CAN SEE.

SOMETIMES TEN YEARS, SOMETIMES THIRTY...WORLDWIDE CROP FAILURE, DROUGHT-- SO MANY THINGS.

ALL THAT METHANE, ALL THAT CARBON DIOXIDE...BUT THE FIGURES COULD CHANGE.

NOTHING IS DECIDED YET. I SEE PATHS FORKING OFF IN MANY DIFFERENT DIRECTIONS, SOME OF THEM UNTHINKABLE, OTHERS JUST UNACHIEVABLE.

WE NEED TO CHOOSE OUR PATH AND FIGHT FOR IT, WITH EVERYTHING WE'VE GOT... BEFORE THAT ROAD IS CLOSED OFF TO US FOR GOOD.

RIGHT NOW, THE METHANAUR IS *THE BIGGEST* AND MOST IMMEDIATE THREAT TO OUR FUTURE.

SO FIRST, WE NEED TO STOP THE GUY WHO'S PRACTICALLY EXCAVATING THE METHANAUR FROM THE ICE WITH THE ENVIRONMENTAL DAMAGE HIS COMPANY IS CAUSING.

AND WHO'S THAT?

JASON GREENLEAF.

EASE UP, MAN. PEOPLE ARE GONNA START NOTICING.

AMAZINGLY, THAT'S NOT HELPING ME STAY CALM.

OH!

THIS IS IT, RIGHT? GOD, PLEASE DON'T BE LOCKED...

SE 5.06

GIVE IT A TRY, OR DO I HAVE TO WATCH YOU PULL YOUR BACK OUT AGAIN?

HA HA...

YES! OKAY, WE'RE GOOD.

RIGHT, YOU'RE LOOKING FOR ANYTHING ABOUT THE BIOFUELS.

BLUEPRINTS, BUDGETS, RESEARCH--ANY EVIDENCE THAT GREENLEAF KNEW THE DAMAGE THEY WERE CAUSING.

DOUBLE TAP YOUR GOGGLES-- THEY GO INTO NIGHT MODE.

OKAY, NOW I'M STARTING TO FEEL COOL...

SO, ER, SHILPA CALLED TO ASK ABOUT LEON.

I SAID WE HADN'T HEARD ANYTHING. HOW LONG DO WE GIVE IT?

BUT WHAT DO WE DO, MO?

TELL THE POLICE THAT OUR FRIEND WENT MISSING AFTER BREAKING INTO A BILLIONAIRE'S PRIVATE OFFICE?

SO...EVEN THOUGH HE COULD BE IN TROUBLE, WE LIE LOW?

LEON WOULD HAVE UNDERSTOOD.

LEON

NO NEW MESSAGES

LEON! YOU GOT OUT SAFELY! BUT...HOW?

WITH INGENUITY... AND A BIT OF CHARM.

IT WENT A LITTLE SOMETHING LIKE THIS...

HEY YOU! YOU SHOULDN'T BE HERE!

PIZZA DELIVERY!

I'M LOOKING FOR THE...

...NORTHEAST WING?

MONTHS LATER, GREENLEAF'S AIRFIELD

THAT'S WHY WE HAVE TO DO THIS.

THAT'S WHY WE HAVE TO FIGHT.

The Daily Wail

WIN! £300,000 lawnmower!

RENEGADES WREAK RUNWAY HAVOC!

Snowflake protesters don't care that you have a flight to catch

WOULD YOU MIND JUST SAYING A FEW WORDS ABOUT WHAT THIS OCCUPATION MEANS TO YOU?

SURE. IT MEANS SHOWING THE WORLD THAT CLIMATE CHANGE IS REAL.

--AND LETTING BUSINESS OWNERS LIKE JASON GREENLEAF OFF THE HOOK, THINGS WILL GET WORSE.

IT MEANS ACKNOWLEDGING THAT IF WE CARRY ON PUMPING GREENHOUSE GASES INTO THE ATMOSPHERE AND CHOPPING DOWN FORESTS--

IT MEANS ACKNOWLEDGING THAT IT MIGHT ALREADY BE TOO LATE, BUT THAT IT'S STILL WORTH TRYING.

IT MEANS MAKING A STATEMENT ABOUT RESPONSIBILITY.

POWERFUL WORDS, PROFESSOR KATELYN. THANK YOU FOR YOUR TIME.

WHAT THE...*KATELYN?!*

IT MEANS A PERSON WHO REJECTS SOCIETY AND GOES IT ALONE. OR A--

RENEGADES. THEY'RE CALLING US RENEGADES! WHAT'S THAT SUPPOSED TO MEAN?

THE KULANDANS...

JASON GREENLEAF TOOK AWAY *OUR* LAND. HE TOOK AWAY *OUR* HOME. ALL SO HE COULD MAKE A PROFIT FROM HIS PLANTATION.

BUT HE WASN'T THE ONLY ONE. THEY CALLED IT THE LANDRUSH.

ALL THOSE BILLIONAIRES MAKING BIDS ON LAND THAT WASN'T RIGHTFULLY THEIRS, AND YOUR GOVERNMENT JUST SAT THERE!

LOOK AT ALL OF YOU--SO-CALLED POLICE, SECURITY! WHERE WERE YOU WHEN WE LOST WHAT WAS RIGHTFULLY OURS?

WE ARE DEFIANT!

WE LOST *EVERYTHING*. BUT WE REBUILT OUR HOME IN THE MEMORY OF THOSE WE LOST THAT DAY, ACCORDING TO THE SPIRIT THEY LIVED BY.

KULANDU ISN'T JUST A PLACE-- IT'S A *DREAM* OF A BETTER WAY OF LIFE. AND NOW WE ARE BRINGING THAT DREAM HERE.

...BUT I HAD A HEAD START ON YOU!

ALSO, MO, WE COULD USE THAT DISTRACTION SOON. THE METHANAUR IS GETTING A BIT...*RESTLESS* WITH US RUNNING ALL OVER IT...

I'M IN POSITION, KATE. NOW WHAT?

THE SHIELD IS LIKE LEON'S SUIT--IT'S IN TUNE TO YOUR BODY, SO IT SHOULD WORK FOR YOU. I DON'T KNOW EXACTLY HOW, BUT--

GREAT, EASY...

WELL, LET'S SEE... PERHAPS IF I FOCUS MY MIND...

WHOA!

WHOOSH

IT *WORKED!*

I GOT ITS ATTENTION. IT'S FOLLOWING ME!

OH MY GOD--IT'S FOLLOWING ME...

BREAKING: ECOTERRORISTS DISTURB METHANE-BREATHING MONSTER

NEWS

CLIMATE ACTIVISTS HAVE RELEASED FOOTAGE OF AN UNPROVOKED ATTACK ON A CREATURE KNOWN AS A "METHANAUR."

CREATURE KNOWN AS "METHANAUR" PROVOKED BY KNOWN CLIMATE PROTESTORS

THEIR MOTIVATIONS ARE CURRENTLY UNCLEAR, BUT LOCAL AUTHORITIES SUSPECT THIS MAY BE AN ACT OF ECO-TERRORISM.

BACK IN LONDON

UH...I THINK SOMETHING MIGHT HAVE BEEN LOST IN TRANSLATION.

LEON, DOES RENEGADES SOUND SO BAD TO YOU NOW?

YOU KNOW WHAT THEY SAY--"NO GOOD DEED GOES UNPUNISHED," OR WHATEVER.

HEY, BUT AT LEAST WE'RE NOT THE *ONLY ONES* ON THE RUN!

GREENLEAF UNDER INVESTIGATION

BILLIONAIRE JASON GREENLEAF'S COMPANY IS BEING INVESTIGATED FOR FRAUD AND THE ILLEGAL DESTRUCTION OF ENDANGERED RAIN FOREST LAND--

SEEMS LIKE WE'RE GOING TO HAVE TO HUNKER DOWN FOR A WHILE.

BUT AT LEAST THIS TIME WE'RE NOT RUNNING ANYMORE.

YEAH, I'M DONE RUNNING NOW. BECAUSE WHAT MATTERS IS WE *CAN* MAKE A DIFFERENCE. WE HAVE A PROMISE TO KEEP, TO THE PLANET, TO MANKIND, TO--

AHEM.

AH...UH, HI, AMBER!

HONESTLY, FOR WANTED CRIMINALS, YOU'RE ALL VERY EASY TO FIND. I'VE ONLY JUST GOT BACK TO THE UK MYSELF, AND ALREADY I HAVE TWO BONES TO PICK WITH ALL OF YOU.

FIRST, YOU'RE WANTED BY *SEVEN* DIFFERENT COUNTRIES?!

WE CAN EXPL--

AND EVEN WORSE, NONE OF YOU DID THE ONLINE THERAPY I GAVE YOU! SO, GO ON--WHO'S GOING TO TELL ME *WHAT* IS GOING ON?!

I DESERVE AN EXPLANATION IF I'M GOING TO BE HARBORING SO-CALLED *TERRORISTS* IN MY WORKPLACE!

WELL...IT'S A LONG STORY...

THE END.

THE CLIMATE EMERGENCY

WHILE A GIANT METHANAUR MAY BE A WORK OF FICTION, THE THREAT OF CLIMATE CHANGE IS VERY REAL AND AFFECTS US ALL. TO HAVE ANY CHANCE OF PREVENTING THE PLANET FROM WARMING FURTHER, WE NEED TO ACT NOW, SO IT'S IMPORTANT TO UNDERSTAND THE SCIENCE OF CLIMATE CHANGE-- THE CAUSES, THE EFFECTS, AND WHAT WE CAN ALL DO ABOUT IT.

WHAT IS CLIMATE CHANGE?

The climate of our planet changes slowly, over long periods of time, but human activity is causing it to warm faster than usual. This is affecting both the climate and life on Earth. For example, when Arctic ice melts, it means a loss of habitat for many animals.

WHY IS IT HAPPENING?

Earth is warmed by a layer of gases in the atmosphere that trap heat from the sun. Many human activities release gases, such as carbon dioxide and methane, known as greenhouse gases because they build up in the atmosphere trapping more heat, like the glass of a greenhouse.

WHAT ARE THE CAUSES?

Rising consumption is increasing the demand for energy to power industry and our homes, for transportation, and for food. Burning fossil fuels (coal, oil, and gas), deforestation, and farming all emit greenhouse gases. The actions of the super-rich—such as traveling in private jets, like Jason Greenleaf's—can be especially harmful. The average private jet flight emits around 150 times more greenhouse gases than a similar journey by high-speed train.

WHAT ABOUT BIOFUELS?

Fuels made from plants are called biofuels. When they burn, they emit greenhouse gases, but this is offset to some degree by the fact that they absorb carbon dioxide as they grow. Biofuels used to be considered a more sustainable alternative to fossil fuels, but they are often the cause of severe deforestation.

WHY ARE FORESTS IMPORTANT?

Forests are known as "carbon sinks" because trees take in and store carbon dioxide to get energy. When a forest is cleared and burned—for grazing cattle or growing biofuels for example—not only is this carbon dioxide released into the atmosphere, but also a carbon sink is lost. Biofuels made of crop waste are therefore much more sustainable than those made of crops grown for biofuel.

WHAT ARE THE CONSEQUENCES?

Climate change is having a big impact on our planet. A rise in temperature of a few degrees might not seem much, but it has caused ice to melt and sea levels to rise. The change in temperature has also led to more extreme weather events, including tropical cyclones like Cyclone Idai in 2019, which tragically killed more than 1,000 people in Mozambique, Zimbabwe, and Malawi.

ARCTIC ICE AND METHANE

Global warming is causing huge areas of ice in the Arctic to melt. Some of this ice forms part of frozen lakes and frozen earth, called permafrost, in which methane gas is trapped. When these areas thaw, methane—a far more potent greenhouse gas than carbon dioxide—is released. This begins a vicious cycle of global warming— as the planet warms, more ice melts and more methane is released.

WHAT CAN WE DO?

We can all take individual action to cut emissions, by eating less meat and using greener ways to travel. But to make a real impact, big companies and governments must act, too. We need to speak up to insist the climate emergency becomes a priority. School strikes, letters to politicians, and peaceful protest are all useful ways we can help make our voices heard. History shows this can lead to victory. Like in our story, plans for an airport near Nantes, France, were scrapped in 2018, due to activists occupying the site with an ecocamp.

MEET THE TEAM

IT'S GOING TO TAKE A SUPERHUMAN EFFORT TO SLOW DOWN CLIMATE CHANGE, SO A TEAM OF STUDENTS AND YOUNG ILLUSTRATORS GOT TOGETHER TO CREATE SOME COMIC BOOK SUPERHEROES TO HELP "SAVE THE WORLD". WE'RE GOING TO NEED ALL THE HELP WE CAN GET!

JEREMY BROWN

THE RENEGADES WAS COFOUNDED BY JEREMY WHILE STUDYING A MASTER'S IN CLIMATE CHANGE AT KING'S COLLEGE LONDON. ALONGSIDE DREAMING UP THE CHARACTERS AND STORY ARCS, HE ENJOYS A SPOT OF POLITICS AND STAND-UP COMEDY.

KATY JAKEWAY

WHILE CREATING THE RENEGADES, KATY WAS ALSO STUDYING AT KING'S COLLEGE LONDON. KATY JOINED THE PROJECT IN ITS EARLY DAYS, USING HER PASSION FOR ART AND WRITING TO HELP BRING JEREMY'S INITIAL IDEAS TO LIFE.

DAVID SELBY

CO-SCRIPTWRITER OF THE RENEGADES AND FELLOW KING'S COLLEGE LONDON STUDENT, DAVID WAS EAGER TO BUILD ON JEREMY AND KATY'S IDEAS AND HOPES TO SEE THE PROJECT RAISE AWARENESS ABOUT CLIMATE CHANGE.

LIBBY REED

LIBBY SPENDS MOST OF HER TIME DRAWING AND MAKING UP STORIES. SHE LOVES ANIMALS, ESPECIALLY REPTILES, AND USES HER ARTWORK TO SHOW THE BEAUTY OF THE NATURAL WORLD.

ELLENOR MERERID

ELLENOR IS INSPIRED BY DAVID ATTENBOROUGH AND CHARLES DARWIN; PEOPLE WHO HAVE SHOWN THE MIGHT AND MIRACLE OF OUR PLANET TO MILLIONS OF PEOPLE. ELLENOR LIKES FOLKLORE AND STARGAZING.

ACKNOWLEDGMENTS SPECIAL THANKS TO SUFFOLK FRIEND AND COMIC GEEK, MISCHA PEARSON, FOR PIONEERING THE GUARDIANS OF THE PLANET (THE PREDECESSOR TO THE RENEGADES). MUCH CREDIT TO COURSEMATES JONATHAN HYDE, TOM HAMBLEY, AND ELIAS YASSIN FOR THEIR GEOGRAPHICAL WISDOM, BOLD ACTIVISM, AND LOYAL FRIENDSHIP, WHICH ALL VERY MUCH HELPED SHAPE THE COMIC. THERE ARE TOO MANY TO LIST HERE, BUT A BIG THANK YOU ALSO TO JAMES PORTER, GEORGE ADAMSON, ODHRAN LINSEY, MICHAEL BARNARD, AND ALL THE LOVELY CREW AT DK FOR THEIR ENTHUSIASM, PATIENCE, AND COMMITMENT TO PROTECTING THE PLANET THROUGH STORYTELLING.

DK WOULD LIKE TO THANK HAZEL BEYNON FOR PROOFREADING